GINA'S SATURDAY ADVENTURE

Rosario De Bello

PAULIST PRESS
NEW YORK AND MAHWAH, N.J.

Library of Congress Cataloging-in-Publication Data

De Bello, Rosario, 1923-
    Gina's Saturday adventure/Rosario De Bello.
       p. cm.
    Summary: After promising her mother she would stay close to home, Gina skates off to the circus with her friend.
    ISBN 0-8091-6612-7 (paper)
    [1. Circus—Fiction.] I. Title.
PZ7.D3537Gi   1993
[Fic]—dc20
                                                 93-5845
                                                  CIP
                                                    AC

Published by Paulist Press
997 Macarthur Boulevard
Mahwah, New Jersey 07430

Printed and bound in the
United States of America

This book is dedicated
to all the Sisters of my Religious community,
The Dominican Congregation of St. Catherine De Ricci
but especially to those Sisters
with whom I have worked and lived
and shared life in its fullness.

One Saturday morning in May, I bounced happily out of bed. Today the circus was coming to town and Dori and I had plans. I hugged my secret to myself. Better not give it away. Mama was sure to guess.

"Hooray!" I shouted. "The sun is shining. What a perfect day to go roller skating."

"Hurry down to breakfast, Gina," Mama called, "or there won't be any playing outside."

When I was a child, living in the big city during the 1930s, it was safe to play on the sidewalks and in the streets. Few cars passed through our streets. The streets were like playgrounds where children played hopscotch, jumped rope or went roller skating. Since there was no T.V., we played outside whenever the weather permitted. Mama liked me to get the fresh air, too. So now I asked her.

"Mama, can I play outside with my roller skates this morning?" She smiled and said, "All right but stay on our side of the street, and do what Maria tells you. When I'm not here she is in charge. I'll be home from work by noon."

Uh oh! Maria in charge! My older sister could be strict. But I wasn't worried. I'd be home by noon. Dori had promised.

Mama pulled her cloche hat over her jet black hair and bustled out to catch the trolley car that took her to work downtown.

Because Maria was fourteen, she liked to show off how grown-up she was. To make sure I knew she was in charge, she made me eat all my oatmeal. Then I had to brush my teeth. Maria also liked to bake.

"Gina, do you want to help me bake those nice ricotta cookies Mama likes?" Maria asked.

"No, I don't. I want to go outside while it's so nice. Please! Can't I go now?" I begged.

Of course, I was thinking of Dori waiting for me. Dori didn't have an older sister to bug her. She was an only child who was spoiled.

"All right, all right," Maria said, "but stay close to the house."

Grabbing my skates, I ran out of the front door. I sat on the white marble steps and quickly put on my skates. Then I pushed on down the street. On and on I went till I screeched to a stop against Mosca's grocery store window. There was Dori reading the sign in the window.

**THE CIRCUS COMES TO
PHILADELPHIA
THE RINGLING BROTHERS BARNUM AND
BAILEY CIRCUS
May 11 to 18, 1932**
Buy tickets now for the Big Tent and Side Show!

"Hi, Dori," I said. "Isn't it a great day to go to the circus?"

"Sure, but I thought you would never make it," she said. "Even though we don't have tickets we can look around at the animals and stuff."

"My mother will be home from work by noon, so remember you promised we'd be back by then," I said.

"I promise again. Cross my heart," she said, tracing a big cross over her chest. "We'll be over and back before then. Why do you have to be such a Mama's girl?"

Being called a Mama's girl upset me but I wanted to go to the circus too much to let Dori bother me. Today I would be as daring as she.

"Let's go, Dori, before I change my mind," I said and off we went up Sixth Street. I waved to Dominic, the shoemaker, as we whizzed by his

shop. The ice-wagon rattled by, pulled by a tired old horse. The number 42 trolley whirred along the tracks as we tried to keep up with it.

We stopped for a rest at the next corner. Ferko's drugstore looked inviting with its tempting signs for a nice cool drink of Coca-Cola. We whisked by Fineman's drygoods store and Schneider's bakery shop. The delicious odor of powdered doughnuts followed us up the street.

At last we came to Erie Avenue. Five more blocks to go to 11th Street where the circus grounds were located. John, the cop, put up his white-gloved hand.

"Where are you headed for in such a hurry, my fine lassies?" he asked with a grin.

"To the circus!" Dori and I chorused.

"To the circus, is it? Watch out for the elephants, don't get trampled on. Be on your way now."

On and on we rolled until we saw the tops of the circus tents. At the entrance, we took off our skates and carried them. Since it was still early, we could walk around and watch the circus crew getting ready for the big opening.

It was like stepping into a dream world. It gave me an eerie yet wonderful feeling. We gaped at the fancy wagons and unusual looking people running thither and yon. Even the smells were different and exciting. There was a mixture of animal odors, sawdust, exotic perfumes, roasting peanuts and caramel candy.

The magic of the moment swept everything else from my mind.

"Gina, look!" said Dori. "Here's the sideshow tent. Let's peep in."

Dori lifted a corner of the flap. We couldn't believe our eyes. A lady with a black beard was talking to a lady who was so fat she looked like a

walking balloon. There was a man so tall he almost touched the top of the tent and there were a lot of little people, smaller than ourselves, with old-looking faces. It was very strange. I pulled on Dori's sleeve, wanting to leave.

Next we ran to the big tent and crept under a loose flap. We saw rows and rows of benches lined around a huge circle in the middle. Workmen were so busy getting the tent ready that they didn't notice us.

There were three rings within the large circle where all the action of the big tent takes place. In the first ring, elephants on their hind legs were bouncing balls on their noses. Horses were galloping around the edge of the ring with riders jumping from horse to horse. In the second ring, a lion tamer was entering a cage of lions. The big cats leaped onto platforms at his command. In the third ring, trapeze artists were doing leaps and somersaults into the air. All this went on at once while the circus band played on to accompany all this movement.

What a thrill, I thought, to be under the big tent where most of the action of a circus takes place. Here we were watching a practice performance. So much was going on at once, I didn't know where to look first. The enthralling sights put all else out of my mind. Coming back to reality, I turned to say something to Dori but she was gone!

"Dori, Dori," I called.

Where could she be? I began running from one tent to another, in hopes of finding her. There was no sign of her. I peeped under the flaps of smaller tents. Under one tent, I saw clowns having their faces painted by a young woman.

"Hi," she said. "Are you lost?"

"Sort of," I said. "I'm looking for my friend. Have you seen her?"

"What does she look like?" asked the young lady.

"She's a little taller than I am and has short blond hair," I said.

"Hmm, I did paint a little girl's face who fits your description, but I don't know where she went," the lady replied.

"Thank you," I said, feeling forlorn. At that moment, I heard a clock striking. It chimed eleven times.

I panicked. Where could Dori be? We would be late getting home if we didn't start now. Oh my! Mama will be so disappointed in me. Why did I ever agree to come with Dori? The fear of crossing the streets alone made me look more diligently for Dori. Just as I gave up hope of finding her, there she was grinning at me from behind a funny clown face.

"Dori," I cried, "where have you been? I've been looking all over for you. We'll be late getting home if we don't start now. You promised we'd be home by noon."

"You're such a Mama's baby, Gina. You'll just have to go home alone. I want to stay and see more of the circus," Dori said as she flounced away.

Dori had never intended to keep her promise, I thought. Now I would have to go home alone and face Mama.

On the verge of tears, I rushed out of the circus grounds. I didn't bother to put on my skates. In my hurry to cross the avenue, I tripped on the trolley tracks and fell, scraping both knees. Blood oozed from the holes in my cotton lisle stockings.

Finally, I reached Erie Avenue. There John, the cop, held up his hand and said, "Here, here, young lady, what happened to you?"

"Oh, John," I cried choking on my tears. "I'm running to get home by noon because Mama doesn't know where I am and I fell and scraped my knees." It all came out in a breathless jumble.

"Well, don't you worry, lass. I'll have you home before you know it. Get in my car and I'll drive you the rest of the way."

I glanced up at John's ruddy face and saw him smiling down at me reassuringly.

"Thank you, John. Maybe I'll get home before Mama does," I said, as I scrambled into the front seat of the police car. For a moment, I was so thrilled to be riding in a police car that I forgot why I was riding in John's car. But it all came

back in a rush. What will Mama say when she sees me coming home in a police car?

Off we went and in no time John was zooming to a stop in front of our little red brick house. There was Mama looking up and down the street.

Oh my, I thought, she really looks worried and upset. Then she saw me getting out of John's police car. Mama's look of shock and alarm made me realize how much anxiety I had caused her.

"Gina," she exclaimed, "what happened to you? Where have you been and why is John bringing you home?"

Trying to answer all her questions at once, I began to explain.

"Oh Mama, I'm sorry! John saw me running to get home and offered me a ride so you wouldn't worry. You see," I gulped as I continued, "I went to the circus grounds with Dori and lost track of the time. I know I disobeyed you and I'm sorry I made you worry. I promise, Mama, I won't do it again."

Seeing my sad tear-streaked face and skinned knees, Mama said gently, "Well, we'll talk about that later after we take care of your knees. Now thank John for bringing you home."

We both thanked John, then Mama took me inside. As she was cleaning my knees, Maria rushed in saying, "It's about time you came home. I should have known you were up to something."

"Hush, Maria. Gina feels bad enough about what she did, and she fell and scraped her knees."

To me Mama said, "But lying wasn't very nice. Anything could have happened." Her voice was stern.

"I know and I'm sorry I lied," I told her.

"Go up to your room now and clean up," she said. "I'll be up in a minute."

I ran upstairs in tears. Mama will never trust me again, I thought.

Soon Mama came up to my room with a cup of hot chocolate.

"There now, Gina, don't cry. I still love you even when you disobey me. Maybe staying in your room for a while will help you to remember not to do it again."

Just then the front doorbell rang. "Gina, Dori is here," called Maria. "Can she come up?"

"Yes, bring her up," said Mama.

"Gee whiz! I'm sorry I got you in trouble, Gina," Dori said as she rushed into the room. "You're lucky to have a mother and sister who worry about you. I wish I did."

"From now on we will worry about you too, Clown Face," said Mama laughing.

Dori's face was hidden by a funny red clown

nose and red, white and blue designs on her cheeks and forehead.

"How about keeping Gina company for lunch? She has to stay in her room for the rest of the day. Maria made some ricotta cookies for dessert. I'm sure both of you are hungry after your morning adventure," Mama smiled knowingly.

Dori grinned. "Thanks, but maybe I'd better wash off my clown face first."